HARRY'S STORMY NIGHT

HARRY'S STORMY NIGHT

UNA LEAVY
ILLUSTRATED BY PETER UTTON

ORCHARD BOOKS

For my husband Lorcan
with love.
U.L.

For Harvey, Lesley and Harriet
P.U.

ORCHARD BOOKS
96 Leonard Street, London EC2A 4RH
Orchard Books Australia
14 Mars Road, Lane Cove, NSW 2066
ISBN 1 85213 526 3 (hardback)
ISBN 1 85213 861 0 (paperback)
First published in Great Britain 1994
First paperback publication 1995
Text © Una Leavy 1994
Illustrations © Peter Utton 1994

The right of Una Leavy to be identified as the Author and Peter Utton as the Illustrator of this
Work has been asserted by them in accordance with the Copyright, Designs and Patents Act, 1988.

A CIP catalogue record for this book is available from the British Library.

Printed in Belgium

All evening, the North wind roared.

Harry had never heard such wind,
whistling over chimneys,
ripping through hedges,
whipping at branches
over his head.

His mother tapped at the window.
"Come in, Harry," she said.
"It's getting very wild
and soon it will be night.
Time to be inside."

It was warm inside,
Baby Tom asleep and
only the storm for noise.

Just then Daddy came in.
"There's a tree down," he said.
"It brought some wires with it,
and the wind is rising. There'll
be no power tonight."

But the stove
glowed brightly,
the kettle began to whistle.
They put candles
in the candlesticks
and settled down
for a long stormy night.

Mum made apple tart.
Harry helped with the pastry,
rolling it this way and that.

All the time
wind boomed at the windows,
branches tapped at the glass.
Baby Tom awoke,
chewing his fingers,
and crying for his food.

Harry held him
while Mum warmed his milk.
His eyes were wide
with the soft mellow light
and the great noise outside.

They washed up after tea
and put the baby to bed.
There was no T.V.
so Harry made his own
pictures instead.

And Mum told him stories
of times long past when
she was a little girl while
outside the wind still whirled
and Harry was sleepy at last.

Into bed then
where Teddy lay
under the bedclothes.
A spatter of rain
dashed at the window pane.
Harry held Teddy close.

All around the room
everything looked strange.
Where was the bookshelf
with Harry's story books?
His robot collection,
his trucks and transformers
- why did they seem to move?

Harry thumped the pillow,
pulled the quilt to his chin.
"Don't be scared, Teddy,"
he said. "I'll just tuck you in."

What was that?
A little cry came
over the roar of the storm.

"Baby Tom's awake!
He'll be scared!"
Harry hopped out of bed.

In the baby's room
there was only
moonlight.

"Don't cry," Harry said.
"It's all right,
it's just a stormy night."

Harry couldn't lift Tom
from his cot
so he sat on the floor
and over the roar of the wind
he began to sing.

Then he told him stories
as shadows drifted past
while outside
the wind still whirled
and Baby Tom
was sleepy at last.

That's what Mum saw
when she hurried upstairs
and opened the door -
Baby snug in his cot,
Harry asleep on the floor.

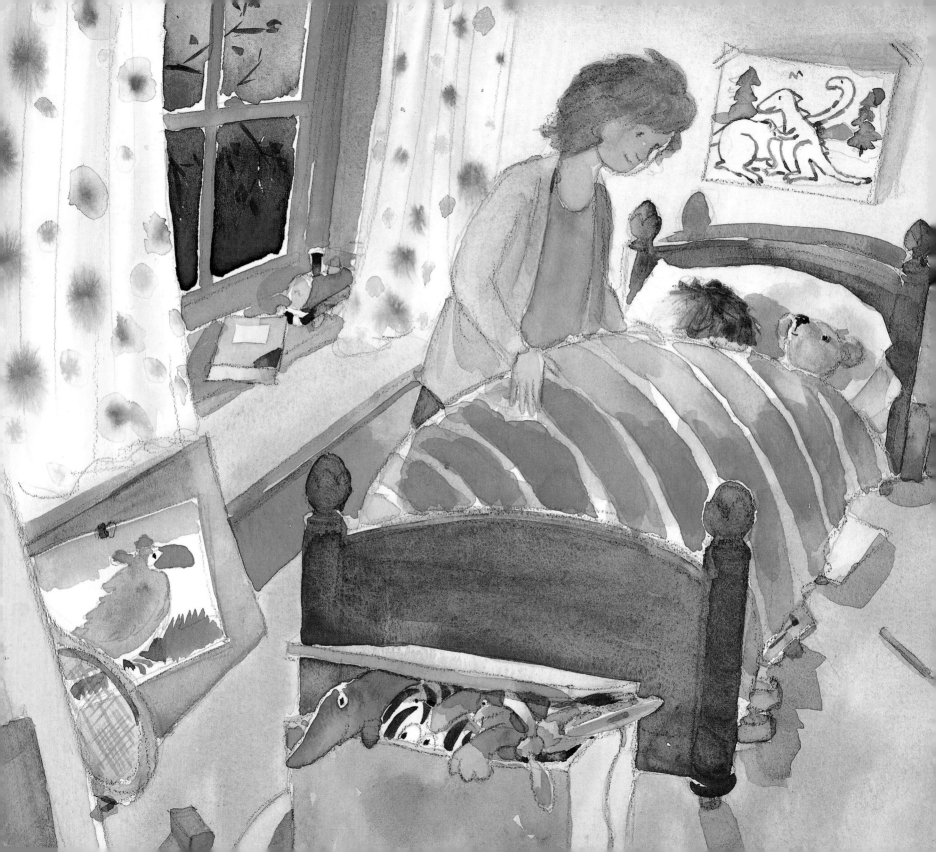

Mum smiled
as she tucked up her boys.
It was warm inside,
the children asleep

and only the storm for noise.